Diary

Stephanie's

Lloyd Williams

ISBN: 978-1-4834-2667-9 (sc)
ISBN: 978-1-4834-2666-2 (e)

Because of the dynamic nature of the Internet, any web addresses or links contained in this book may have changed since publication and may no longer be valid. The views expressed in this work are solely those of the author and do not necessarily reflect the views of the publisher, and the publisher hereby disclaims any responsibility for them.

Any people depicted in stock imagery provided by Thinkstock are models, and such images are being used for illustrative purposes only.
Certain stock imagery © Thinkstock.

Lulu Publishing Services rev. date: 03/10/2015

Chapter 1

February 16, 2002

On a cold Saturday night in Long Island, NY, my mother came home from the bar with a man I had never met. This was no surprise, though. From experience, I knew that he was her drug supplier for the evening—she was about to get high.

"Stephanie, this is my new friend. We met tonight at the bar up the street," my mother said, her eyes darting from me to him.

I glanced out the window and saw the busybodies, Mrs. Scott and Mrs. Andrews. In two strides, I was at the windows, whipping the curtains closed. My mother's drug problem was out of control.

She used to be such a responsible mother, and so attractive. She had been an up-and-coming model, with an endorsement deal for Victoria's Secret on the table. When I was younger, people used to give her compliments all the time. Intimidated by her beauty, men would resort to sneering and catcalling, just to get her attention. Long ago, those modeling agencies had considered her the embodiment of glamour. But after a while, drug abuse took over and she neglected her health. Agencies and investors started to label her a liability.

That was years ago. Her addiction had only worsened over time. Now, as I turned from the window, I realized that she hardly looked the same as she had a month ago. Her dependency on drugs was so bad that even her physical features were deteriorating. Mark, our neighbor of seven years, had called the police a couple of weeks ago, assuming that she was a potential burglar lingering in our backyard.

Watching your mother become a drug addict right before your eyes was devastating, but my mother was also promiscuous. It became a way of life for her: go out, meet a guy, then bring him home. Sex, in exchange for dope. And more dope. And more.

One evening, my mother had a bad reaction to dope, and I had to call the ambulance. I thought she was going to die. She was in a coma for two days. Her heart stopped twice while she was hooked up to the respirator, but miraculously, she survived.

It could have been a wake-up call for her, a chance to start fresh. But we weren't so lucky. In fact, her addiction only got worse after that. I began to notice a pattern in her behavior, and I was afraid that, one day, she would overdose, and my brothers and I would lose her for good.

"Stephanie, did you hear what I just said?" My mom snapped her fingers in front of my face, interrupting my thoughts.

"I heard you, Mother." I rolled my eyes. What was I, a fucking dog?

In the last three days, this was the third man she had brought home.

Home. I had once been happy to call this place *home*, but now it seemed more like a halfway house. My mother was completely unreliable and erratic. The majority of the time, food was scarce because she used the welfare money to support her habit, which kept her from suffering from withdrawal symptoms. Heroin had stolen the mother I'd once known.

And these creeps were coming over so often that I feared not only for my safety, but also for the safety of my brothers. I was sixteen, the middle child. My seventeen-year-old brother, Tony, had dropped out of school at fifteen. He did whatever he had to in order to keep us afloat. He was probably out holding up a gas station with some local gang members at that very moment. Thank goodness, Stanley was sleeping over his friend Jeremy's house.

"Clean up this mess, Stephanie." She gestured toward the pile of dirty clothes in the corner. "And don't wander off."

After she took the man into her bedroom, I counted to ten. By the time I reached *eight*, I heard banging and moaning emanating from her bedroom.

This was so disgusting!

Was I the only one who had to deal with this sort of thing? I wondered if any of my friends were going through similar situations. Maybe they kept it to themselves, as I did. Maybe we all had secrets. I laughed at myself as I plopped onto the couch and turned on the TV. I couldn't really ask my friends, now could I? Secrets weren't based on trust; they were based on shame.

Chapter 2

The noise from my mother's bedroom had finally ceased. I assumed the man had gotten his thrill and was about to leave. After a few minutes, the door slowly opened, and he appeared in the doorway. A grin slid over his mocha-colored face. The moment I saw him, I was uncomfortable, but the expression on his face heightened my level of discomfort. He had a creepy aura about him.

He stood there, looking at me seductively with glassy eyes. No words were spoken.

Then he walked over.

Initially, I ignored him, focusing intently on my nails; I didn't want to give him a reason to talk. My aloofness only seemed to pique his interest, though.

"May I join you?" he asked.

I glared at him.

Despite my cold demeanor, he took a seat on the shabby brown sofa. Originally, the sofa in my living room had been beige, but through years of neglect and countless stains, the shade had deepened to the color of dirty snow. The sofa was large enough to seat four or five people, so why was he sitting shoulder-to-shoulder beside me? I smoothed my hand over my skirt and willed myself to stop shaking.

His first words sent chills running up my spine—those three words would haunt me for quite some time.

"Are you ready?" he whispered.

I hunched over and started shoving at my cuticles, acting as if I hadn't heard him. Maybe then he would leave me alone, even though that ploy hadn't worked the first time. We sat in awkward silence for about ten seconds.

"Why aren't you in there with my mother?" I finally said. I pointed in the direction of her bedroom, trying to redirect his attention.

"She's no fun at the moment." That slimy grin drifted over his face again. This guy was really weird—and too close for comfort.

Just as I was getting ready to stand up, he put his arm around my shoulder. And squeezed.

"What the hell are you doing?" I asked, hoping he didn't hear the tremor in my voice.

"Are you ready?" he repeated, his tone even deeper than before, his face even closer.

"Ready for what? What the fuck are you talking about? Get away from me!" I shouted. That would grab my mother's attention. Oh, God, don't let her be too high; don't let her be oblivious yet.

Nobody came to my rescue.

The man started to become irate and shout. I got so intimidated, I peed myself a little.

His face scrunched up at the smell. "What the fuck? Did you—" His expression suddenly cleared, as if he had discovered the meaning of life. "Kinky girl. You like to make a mess, huh?" Then he leered at me as if this was the biggest turn-on.

I'd been embarrassed at first, but then I was repulsed. "I'm pretty neat, actually," I stammered. "So I'm gonna go clean up."

"I'll clean you up, baby. Daddy will clean you up real good."

Acting casual, I tried to ease out of his grip.

"Stop playing stupid with me, bitch. A deal is a deal," he shouted in my face. Spittle sprayed my cheek.

A deal is a deal? What was he talking about? Now I was really frightened. If this was some kind of joke, it was in bad taste. But he truly seemed to be upset, as if I owed him something. This was no joke.

It must be a misunderstanding. I tried to still my racing heart and find a measure of calm. "Sir, what are you talking about?" I asked cordially.

The diplomacy of my delivery made no difference. He had already made up his mind to do what he'd set out to do.

"I don't have time for games, so pull down your panties, and I can be on my way," the man said. He mauled my private area. I batted his hand away and tried to push him off, but to no avail. Eventually, he subdued me. He shoved his filthy hand under my skirt and tore my panties off of me.

"Mom! Help me!"

February 16, 2002

Dear Diary,

Tonight, I am no longer a virgin because I was raped. I did not see it coming, but I will never forget his face. He made me keep eye contact with him the entire time I performed oral sex. I felt helpless. I was powerless in comparison to him; there was nothing I could do to stop it from happening. I screamed for help, but my mother didn't come to my rescue. I guess getting high was more important than saving her daughter from being raped. I stayed in the shower for nearly two hours. I feel so dirty. My life is ruined.

Chapter 3

I heard the squeak of my bedroom door as someone walked in unannounced. I was so scared, my teeth began to chatter, or maybe I was just freezing cold; the house felt like an ice box. I wrapped my blanket tighter around me. The footsteps were light and quiet, moving at a very slow pace. Sneaking. He was coming back. He was going to violate me a second time. Paralyzed with fear, I recalled his face looming in front of me and felt his hands around my throat, choking me until I was an inch away from blacking out. A cold sweat smothered my skin.

My world was coming to an end. Again.

Bullshit!

Suddenly determined to fight for my freedom, I whipped the blanket away and sprang out of bed.

The room was empty. Thank God.

"Just a dream," I whispered into the darkness as I lowered myself onto the mattress. But not a dream—a memory. I moaned out loud; the pain was unbearable, and it was everywhere, mind and body, from head to toe. I smoothed my hair out of my face and winced at the contact; that sadistic junkie had pulled my hair until my scalp bled. Of course, I had bled in other places, too. The bastard hadn't seemed concerned about bodily fluids last night while forcing himself inside of me. Maybe he didn't know about this stuff, but I knew. I always paid attention at those assemblies in school; I didn't want to end up like my mother. And so, I was praying that I wouldn't catch any STDs from him.

Never in a hundred years could I have imagined being the victim of such a loathsome crime. I did not want to become part of a statistic, one of countless women who had been victimized. Maybe I should go to the authorities. I had been a virgin when that man sat next to me on the sofa. Now, that once-in-a-lifetime moment was ruined; I could no longer save myself for my husband, because my innocence had been stolen from me. I had to do something. I had to tell someone. He deserved to be punished for this!

And yet, I couldn't help feeling like it was my fault. Even though I tried my best to fight him off, I should have done more. I felt worthless. I hated myself for not being able to stop him. I felt depressed to the point that I was entertaining suicidal thoughts. I decided not to pursue them, mainly because I loved my brothers. I didn't want them to suffer the trauma of finding me dead from having slit my wrists.

Chapter 4

A couple of hours later, my older brother was calling my name. Tony was overly protective of me. If he had walked in on me being raped last night that bastard's family would have been making funeral arrangements this morning.

"Stephanie, wake up," he said as he playfully tugged on my blanket.

I pretended to sleep because I was in no mood to be social. I couldn't even face my own reflection; how could I face Tony?

Then I smelled the aroma of eggs and sausage, which made me reconsider. My stomach was empty. I hadn't eaten since noon of the previous day, and I'd thrown up that little bit after...

I rolled over, pulling the blanket up to my chin, and opened one eye. "Good morning, Tony." I wish I could have sounded half as cheerful as my brother, but I just couldn't do it.

"I got your favorite: sausage, egg, and cheese on an egg bagel with some orange juice from the bodega." He placed the breakfast on my night table.

"Thank you." My tone managed to sound a little more welcoming this time.

"Anytime," he said, gently patting me on my arm before walking out and shutting the door behind him.

My brother was sweet and charming, a virtual stud in our neighborhood. The girls his age and even women much older were always flirting with him. He drew them, without even trying; he was a pretty boy with a tough streak. And that tough streak wasn't really too tough; he considered himself the ultimate player, but his only vice was selling a bit of dope in the neighborhood to make a couple of dollars that would put food on our dinner table.

Another lure for the ladies was his maturity. His crew consisted of men at least ten years his senior. He didn't mingle with his peers because they lacked the discipline and wisdom that he himself had. He made more money than them, helped with more gang-related activities than them, and had a higher ranking than them. So much popularity, though, was sure to breed jealousy.

Chapter 5

After eating breakfast, I gathered enough energy to finally get out of bed. I carefully fixed my hair, then pulled on sweatpants and a turtleneck to cover the fingerprint bruises on my neck.

On my way down the hall, I bumped into my mother, who was leaving the bathroom. She looked awful. Her hair was disheveled, as if she hadn't brushed it in days. Since she was wrapped in a towel, I could see that she had lost a significant amount of weight. Her bones were actually thrusting against her skin, giving her a ghoulish appearance.

"Mother, I need to talk to you," I said, clenching my fist.

"I don't have time right now." She tried to walk past me.

If she thought I was going to forget about what had happened, she had another thing coming. I remembered the man's words from last night; they had reverberated in my head ever since the assault.

A deal is a deal.

I would never forget those words. And my mother would never forget the beating that I was about to deliver to her. I didn't want to believe that my own mother, no matter how neglectful she was, would offer me up for sex, just so she could get high. But her addiction had become so much worse over the past few months; she must not have been thinking rationally to begin with.

Her current behavior was a perfect example; she was stubbornly trying to shove her way past me while clutching the towel, even though I was easily blocking her path with just one hand. She looked like a Chihuahua trying to force its way past a husky. Finally, I had to step in front of her and get in her face so she would listen to me.

"Your junkie friend raped me last night, and he said he paid for me with—"

I didn't see it coming; she slapped me in the face before I could even finish my sentence. Releasing her grip on the towel, she wrapped her hands around my throat and pinned me against the wall. Shock held me immobile. Fear quickly followed, as she applied enough pressure with her thumbs to let me know she was serious. In that moment, as I was gasping for breath, I knew she was capable of killing me—if I let her.

"You listen here, you little bitch, and you listen clear," she snarled, looking me in the eyes. "I need my fix, so if that means putting what you have between your legs on the market every once in a while, it is what it is."

The reality of her words cut through me like a blade. She stepped back, covered herself with the towel, and glared at me like a rabid dog. All I could do was walk away from her with my hand pressed against my face, stunned by the vicious encounter.

Chapter 6

I could not believe my mother had permitted a man to sexually violate me. All I could do was hope that it didn't get worse. I vowed that, if I found myself in a similar situation, I would fight or kill anyone who attacked me again.

"Good morning," my younger brother chirped as I shuffled into the kitchen.

Stanley was adorable. He was thirteen years old with curly hair and dimples. He was a younger version of Tony, at least regarding his gestures and phrases. They didn't really look alike, because they didn't share the same father.

"Good morning, Stanley," I said, forcing a smile onto my face.

He walked over and gave me a big hug. At least someone loved me!

"How are you today?" he asked.

Devastated. Heartsick. Broken. "I'm okay."

There was no way I could tell either brother about what had happened last night, but especially not Stanley. They didn't need to know the explicit details, and I didn't need to remind myself of them.

"Did you get your breakfast from Tony?" He walked back to the table and popped the last bite of his sandwich into his mouth.

"Yes. It was very nice of him," I said.

"You don't have to boil hot water today, because Tony went to the gas station early this morning and got some diesel fuel. That should hold us over for a few weeks," Stanley said.

"That's great," I said. Thank God. I wasn't looking forward to washing up like some uncivilized clod.

Whenever we ran out of hot water, we would boil water on the stove and use it for washing up. Tony took the initiative whenever he could. Thanks to his generosity, we wouldn't be subjected to that form of degradation, at least for a few weeks. Tony took his title of *man of the house* seriously; whenever we needed something done, he would put our needs before his. I'm not sure where he learned so much about responsibility and sacrifice, but he certainly took those lessons to heart!

Chapter 7

The day went by quickly; I wasn't ready to see anyone, so I spent the whole time in my room, reading. Now it was evening time. I was an avid reader. Teachers always told me that was why I had a broad vocabulary for my age. I had started reading the dictionary when I was twelve, so I could comprehend the unfamiliar words in my novels. That evening, I finished an awesome Donald Goines book entitled *Daddy Cool*; then I started another book, *I Know Why the Caged Bird Sings*, by Maya Angelou. She was one of my favorite authors; I loved feeling like a fly on the wall as I read her stories. She seemed so genuine and down to earth—the ideal person to meet over a cup of coffee.

I was reading the scene in which Maya has an excruciating toothache and Momma has to take her to the dentist see Dr. Lincoln, when someone knocked on my bedroom door.

After folding the page to save my place in the novel, I said, "Come in. It's open."

Tony stepped into the room. "Stephanie, you wanna get a quick bite to eat?"

Twice in one day? I should take advantage of whatever boon had struck, but I didn't think I would make good company. "Can I take a rain check on this one?"

He frowned. "You aren't hungry?"

"No, it's not that." Self-consciously, I adjusted the collar of my turtleneck. "I'm just feeling a little lethargic today."

His brows shot up at the new vocab word. "Okay. Do you want me to bring you back something?"

"Sure. A slice of pizza would be fine. Thanks, Tony."

After he left, I eagerly continued reading. I really enjoyed a good story, and once I got hold of a good book, I would tune everything out. For me, reading was therapeutic, as well as fundamental. Most kids my age didn't even like school, but I loved to learn. School was my safe haven, an escape from my private life. I always dreaded the weekends; I couldn't wait to go back to school tomorrow.

I had just become engrossed in the plot again when I heard my door slowly open. Without raising my eyes from the page, I asked, "Did you forget how to knock?"

The laughter was cold and unfamiliar.

My gaze flew to the door. No. Not again.

This was a different man. He was white, with long dirty nails and bad teeth. His lack of hygiene made me instantly nauseous.

He came toward me.

I kept backing away from him, across the bed. Then I fell onto the floor, landing on my wrist. Pain rocketed through me, but still, I jumped to my feet. "What the hell are you doing in here?"

"You must be Stephanie." Towering over me, he licked his lips.

"Get the hell out before my brothers get back!"

My false bravado didn't even make him blink. There was no fear in his eyes, no concern—just unwavering lust. I knew in my heart that my mother had arranged this.

Lloyd Williams

February 17, 2002

Dear Diary,

I tried to fight him. I kicked. I screamed. I wanted to kill him. But he was choking the life out of me. He raped me. He raped me. And right before he left, he told me to thank my mother. He'd never had a minor before.

I've always believed in God, but I don't know if there is a God out there anymore. So I'm going to pray, and if you can hear me, can you please stop this from happening to me? It's not fair! I'm a good girl. I always stay out of trouble, and that's not easy, living around here. There are plenty of bad people around here, and drugs and gangs are making things worse. I don't wish this on nobody, but, if there is a God out there listening, please have an angel watch over me and my brothers. PLEASE!

18

Chapter 8

The next morning, when I was getting ready for school, my thoughts traveled back to last night. I had to race into the bathroom to throw up. After brushing my teeth, I looked in the mirror. I looked like... oh, god, I looked like my mother, with these bags under my eyes. But what could I expect when I had hardly slept for the past two nights?

I had to get out of the house!

* * * * *

I arrived at school an hour later.

"Hey, Stephanie!" My good friend Emily ran over to me and gave me a hug. People often complained about how long-winded she could be, but Emily was just sociable. I was the antithesis of her. In fact, I was so reserved that people often forgot I was in the room.

"Hey," I replied, returning the hug.

She stepped back and grinned. "I had the most amazing weekend. Remember my cousin Michelle? The one I haven't seen in years?" She waited for me to nod, then continued, "She showed up on the doorstep Friday night!"

"Was she okay? Did she get kicked out?"

"No!" Emily laughed. "She just came over to surprise me! We hung out all weekend. It was awesome! I wish you could have met her, Stephanie. How about you? What did you do?"

"Nothing much." I could feel my stomach churning again. "Let's talk later. I need to stop in the ladies' room."

"I'll come with you, girl." She fell into step beside me.

No way. She'd want to talk about my weekend. I needed to avoid her at all costs. At least for the moment.

"No! It's not that type of bathroom run," I explained, desperation straining my voice.

She stopped walking and frowned at me. "Stephanie, are you okay?"

Was she seeing right through me? I stood beside her, bouncing on my toes a bit with impatience. "I have to do a number two," I explained. That would surely get her to leave me alone. I even went as far as to put my hand on my bottom, to emphasize my level of emergency.

"Okay. Well, you go take care of that issue," she said as she backed away and waved goodbye.

I suddenly pictured the dictionary I had read a few years ago. The revised version would probably have my picture next to the word *pathetic.*

Chapter 9

"Are there any questions?" Mr. Philips asked in his typical, listless tone. He was a man who no longer had a passion for his profession.

This was the last class of the day. It was an honors class, and I'd been having trouble with some math equations, so I had asked Mr. Philips if I could stay after for help.

The bell rang. Most students loved the sound of the bell; half of them had already left the room by the time I'd closed my math book and graph notebook. The way I viewed it, that bell meant I was one step closer to being home and putting up with my mother's crap. I wasn't in a rush to go somewhere that was so unsafe.

"Stephanie, are you ready?" Mr. Philips followed the last student to the doorway, then closed the door.

All of my classmates had rushed out of the classroom so quickly, eager to go about their lives. But I was going about my life, too. I was going to maintain my 4.0 GPA. I was going to do something with my life. I just needed a little help with the honors class.

"Thanks again for staying to help me, Mr. Philips," I said as I opened up my folder and pulled out the sheet of equations.

He walked over to my desk. "My pleasure. So what math problems do you find to be hard?"

Oddly, he seemed to emphasize the word *hard*. I hope he didn't think I was pretending to have trouble. Some kids did that because they were lazy; it was easier to say the work was too hard than to spend some time figuring it out.

I showed him the examples that I had struggled with. Before long, I started to get the hang of them. It was much easier to understand when we went over a few at a slower pace. Sometimes, in class, he moved so quickly that I had trouble writing everything down.

"You're doing great," Mr. Philips said, as he patted me on the shoulder.

He glanced toward the door, then his hand slid slowly from my shoulder to the middle of my back, and then further down.

I glared up at him, disapproval written all over my face.

"Just relax," he murmured, as he rubbed my back.

I felt uncomfortable, but after everything that had happened over the weekend, maybe I was jumping to conclusions. Then he stepped even closer to me and shifted his hips. The proximity of his crotch to my mouth was unquestionably inappropriate.

He saw me looking, and misinterpreted. "You want to see what's in there?" He gestured to what was starting to take shape inside of his pants.

Mr. Philips was a heavyset man. I had no doubt that I could outrun him. Without further thought, I leapt to my feet and sprinted out of the classroom, leaving behind my property. I heard him call my name and start to follow me.

Just then, another student rounded the corner and bumped into me. When I looked around again, I saw Mr. Philips swiftly retreating into his classroom.

* * * * *

Back at home, I took another long shower and went straight to my room. This latest incident with Mr. Philips was too much for my mind to handle. Why were men gravitating toward me all of a sudden? Did most attractive women go through this kind of abuse? Was it normal?

I just wanted to be left alone. Luckily, no one was home tonight; even Stanley was out, sleeping over his buddy's house. I wandered into the kitchen. The fridge contained a half-empty jar of jam and a carton of spoiled milk. I guess I will not be eating dinner.

I returned to my room and started thinking about why my life was in shambles and how I could improve it. I finally decided that, if I couldn't kill myself and I couldn't get fat, I would have to start standing up for myself. Tomorrow, when I went back to school, I would speak with my guidance counselor and lodge a formal complaint against Mr. Philips. That should solve one problem. As for my situation at home, there was really only one solution: I decided to move out.

February 18, 2002

Dear Diary,

Today I stayed after school for extra help, and my math teacher, Mr. Philips, acted very inappropriately. He tried to push up on me, so I had to run out of the classroom. Recently, I got down on my knees and asked god for guidance, but he don't love me. Maybe I should take that as a sign. Now I see why people commit suicide.

Why am I being targeted by these men? What am I doing wrong?

Chapter 10

I was a little nervous the next morning when I arrived at school, but I was determined to get my life on track. The first thing I did was go my counselor's office.

"How can I help you?" the lady at the front desk asked politely.

"My name is Stephanie. Can I speak to Mrs. Thompson?"

She studied the calendar on her desk before responding. "I don't see an appointment, but you can tell me what it is in regard to, and I can schedule an appointment for you."

No way. What if I lost my nerve? Or changed my mind? "This is urgent! It's in regard to an incident that happened yesterday after school, and I cannot stress enough how important this is." I heard a fair amount of desperation in my voice. Would that improve my chances or worsen them?

The woman frowned and took a closer look at me. "Have a seat, Stephanie, while I let Mrs. Thompson know you are here with an emergency."

I sat for several minutes. The more I contemplated the matter, the more I felt like what had happened yesterday was partially my fault. After all, I was the one who had asked for help. And I did look at his crotch when he moved it so close to my face. Totally confused at this point, I stood up to leave.

That was when Mrs. Thompson stepped out of her office. "Stephanie, I haven't seen you in a while. How can I help you?" she asked, while ushering me into her office.

Mrs. Thompson and my family had some history. A year ago, when my brother Tony suddenly stopped attending school, Mrs. Thompson tried to contact my mother to find out what was happening, but she could not reach her over the phone. So she showed up to my house, unannounced. I don't think I'll ever forget the look on her face when she walked inside. Disgust, horror, and pity rarely blend quite so smoothly. She said that our living conditions were deplorable, and she called my mother an unfit parent. But she didn't report us. I never understood her reasoning for that omission. Sometimes, I really wish she had reported us. Then, maybe we'd be safe and fed. Most of the time, though, I was glad that she hadn't; I might have been separated from Stanley and Tony. I couldn't live with that.

I wanted to fully unload, to tell her that those "deplorable living conditions" had gotten a lot more deplorable. But I'd start off small today. As I sat down, I took a deep breath, then began telling Mrs. Thompson about the events that had led to my arrival at her office that morning. At first, she just sat there, looking at me without saying a word; then, she shocked the hell out of me.

"Stephanie, Mr. Philips is one of the best teachers we have, and it would be a shame to lose him. By the same token, it would be a shame if I sent Child protective services to your residence."

I must have misunderstood. I was so suspicious of everyone lately. "What is that supposed to mean?" I asked.

"It means that I would hate to see you and your siblings put in foster care," she said.

I glared at this cold-hearted woman and considered my options, while various scenarios played in my mind. But at the end of each one, we didn't live happily ever after. I stood up and walked out of her office.

She called out, "Stephanie, I believe this belongs to you."

When I turned around, I saw her holding up the backpack that I had left in Mr. Philips' classroom yesterday.

Chapter 11

I didn't move out right away, mainly because I had nowhere to go, no money to pay for rent, and no opportunity to earn money. Sometimes, being a kid was a huge disappointment. The traffic of men in the house was increasing, and the caliber of the men was decreasing (I never thought that would be possible!). I actually stepped on a syringe when I was getting out of the shower this morning.

I was getting more desperate to leave than ever. For the past couple of days, I'd been contemplating asking my friend Emily if her older sister would allow me to temporarily move in with them. Nancy, the older sister, was a popular dancer at a local gentlemen's club, so she knew all about doing what you had to do in order to survive. I didn't think she would object to having me stay there until I got myself together. We were like sisters; I've known Emily since we were in kindergarten. And they knew enough about my home life to know that I wouldn't ask for such a favor without a damn good reason. They would understand. Even so, it would take a lot of courage to ask. What if she said *no*? What if she reported me?

On the way to my next class, I passed Mr. Philips, who was standing in the hallway, monitoring the morning flow of students.

"Good morning, Stephanie," he said as I walked past him. I didn't reply; I just continued walking, looking straight ahead. But I felt the hairs on the back of my neck stand on end. Whirling around, I found him still standing there, gawking at me, while biting his bottom lip. I didn't want to imagine the fanciful thoughts he was having.

Gross.

Out of the corner of my eye, I saw Emily amid a crowd of students. I called out, then rushed to catch up to her.

"Stephanie, how are you?" Emily asked, as she leaned in for a hug.

I took a deep breath. "I'm not so great," I admitted.

She studied me for a few seconds, as if trying to gauge what was wrong. "You look like you haven't slept in days," she said softly.

I knew she was referring to the dark circles under my eyes. She was right; I hadn't slept in days. I jumped at every sound, and I was afraid to close my eyes. Whenever I did, I saw the faces of the men who had raped me.

Fuck it. I don't want to live anymore. How should I end my life? I wish I owned a gun so I could blow my brains out. Should I slit my wrist? Nah, too messy. Should I take pills? That way wouldn't be so messy.

My brother was already heartbroken, though, about our living conditions, so maybe I should wait a little longer. Suicide attempt postponed!

Emily pulled me into a fairly empty stairwell, away from the bustling crowd. "Tell me what's wrong," she finally said.

This was so uncomfortable. I didn't really want to burden my friend, but I didn't know who else to turn to. I had tried making a formal complaint to Mrs. Thompson about the simplest of my problems, but she hadn't taken me seriously. Why would the police be any different? I had to tell somebody, though. I couldn't be one of those closet victims; I needed help.

"Tell me what's wrong, Stephanie. Is it your mother's drug problem?" she asked. She was such a good friend and so worried about me that tears slowly started to surface.

Before she could get another word out—and before I changed my mind—I said the words. "I was raped." I was trembling with the effort to hold myself together, but I couldn't stop the tears from streaming down my cheeks.

Emily pulled me into the embrace I've been needing for days.

Then the words came pouring out. I told her everything that had happened recently, starting with the man in the living room and ending with Mrs. Thompson.

I didn't have to ask for a thing; Emily suggested that I come to live with her and her sister.

$$* * * * *$$

A couple of days later, I moved in with Emily. I really hated leaving my brothers, but my safety was in jeopardy; if I didn't leave soon, either someone would kill me or I would kill myself, despite my resolve. But I couldn't tell them that. When they asked me why I was leaving, I just told them that it was difficult for me to stay there. I promised to elaborate one day.

"Hey, girl." Emily's older sister, Nancy, wrapped her arms around me at the door, before I could even drop my luggage. "You're officially part of the family now, so if you need anything, let big sister know."

"Thank you. I appreciate everything you're doing for me."

She pulled back a bit and looked into my eyes. "I heard what happened, and I'm sorry," she said, without going into it any further. Nancy had always been like the big sister I'd never had. I was so lucky that she had agreed to let me stay!

"You go ahead and get settled; I'll talk to you later." She picked up her car keys and headed out the door.

I took a deep, refreshing breath as I looked at my new surroundings. I knew I was in a much better environment; finally, I would be able to sleep peacefully.

February 22, 2002

Dear Diary,

Today, I moved in with my best friend, Emily, and her older sister, Nancy. I am finally in a place where I feel comfortable again. It is such a relief to know that I don't have to worry about my mother's guests putting their hands on me again. I think I will need therapy in the near future, though, if I can ever afford it. Every so often, I wake up sobbing in the middle of the night from violent nightmares. I hope that, one day, I can live a normal existence and somehow find a way to leave my past in the past. (Fingers crossed)

Chapter 12

I couldn't sleep last night. I had been looking forward to my first night at Emily's so much, but every half hour, I woke up in a cold sweat. The dream that kept shattering my peace felt so real. My tears were real every time I bolted up in bed. In the dream, two gunmen demanded that Tony hand over his valuables. When he refused, they shot him in the head. I needed to call and check up on him and Stanley—I had a feeling something was about to go terribly wrong.

*****

First thing in the morning, I took a nice hot shower. When I came out, to my surprise, I found that Nancy had made me and Emily breakfast. All three of us sat at the kitchen table and chatted over bacon, eggs, and toast. This is what family was supposed to be like.

"Stephanie, we are going out later to get something nice to wear to the party. Do you want to come with us?" Nancy asked.

"Yeah, sure," I said. "What's the occasion?"

"Are you serious?" She shook her head in disapproval.

What had I forgotten?

"It's my twenty-first birthday!" Nancy shouted, as both girls screamed in excitement.

"All of the people that matter are going to be there," Emily said with a mouth full of food.

I felt awful for forgetting about Nancy's birthday. Now that I thought about it, I realized that my birthday was approaching, too.

"I'm sorry, Nancy. With everything that's been going on lately, your birthday totally slipped my mind, girl." I stared down at my plate in shame.

When I finally glanced up, I saw the two girls gaping at me as if I were a total moron. Then they laughed good-naturedly.

"It's okay; I understand. But next year, you'd better not forget," Nancy joked, as she stole a strip of bacon off my plate and started eating it.

"Hey! Don't take my bacon!" I pouted.

She shoved the rest of the strip in her mouth, and a smile of bliss appeared on her face.

"There's no rationing here," Emily assured me. "More bacon is in the pan on the stove top."

No rationing. More food. What kind of magical house had I walked into?

After breakfast, I called Tony. It was good to hear his voice, especially after that horrible dream, but I needed to see him for myself. I wanted to meet him and Stanley somewhere—not at his house—but he offered to pick me up at Emily's.

Chapter 13

A horn was blowing outside. I looked out the window and saw a breathtaking luxury car. Maybe it belonged to one of the dozens of men Nancy had wrapped around her finger. Someone was probably stopping by to give her an early gift and wish her a happy birthday.

I walked down the hall. Nancy was sitting at her vanity in her room, brushing her hair. I knocked on the open door. Her eyes met mine in the mirror. "There's someone outside and I think he's here for you," I said, rolling my eyes at her good-naturedly.

"Don't be jealous." She smiled, revealing pearly white teeth.

No chance of that. That last thing I would ever want was a man's attention.

"Who could it be? I'm not expecting anyone at the moment." She stood up and slipped a robe over her tank top and shorts. "I hate when people stop by my place unannounced," she snarled, brushing past me and stomping toward the front door.

Nancy was extremely attractive, with a perfect body. She was short—no; short was too guttural a word; maybe petite or diminutive. Her skin was a beautiful shade of bronze and she had amazing curves, shown off frequently in her form-fitting clothes. She used her looks to get ahead; she thrived on having her way with men. They, in turn, spoiled her to excess: they lavished her with gifts, paid for her travel expenses, and unstintingly gave her both praise and money whenever she wanted it. And she wanted it a lot. Her picture could be found next to the word *metropolitan* in the dictionary. It might be next to a few other words, too.

For example, Nancy wanted to have her cake and eat it, too. Not too long ago, she showed me pictures of at least a half dozen men whom she was currently dating. Unfortunately, they each thought they were in an exclusive relationship with her. Even worse was the fact that most of them were notorious drug dealers. I begged her to be careful; if one of her boyfriends found out that she was two-timing him, she could be in serious danger.

"Now who's the popular one?" Nancy teased as she skipped back inside. "It wasn't one of my guys; your brothers are out there!"

Laughing, Nancy flounced back into her room. I could only scowl at her closed door. Where the hell had Tony gotten that car? As I strode out the front door and down the sidewalk, I entertained many thoughts, most of them negative. I had only been gone for one day, and Tony had rewarded himself with such an expensive automobile already! He had to be selling huge amounts of dope to afford it.

Chapter 14

I walked over to the driver's side of the car.

Tony was wearing a big grin on his face. "Hey, Stephanie, what do you think of my new car?"

"It's very nice, but the last time I checked, you didn't have any credit, so where did you come up with the money to buy it?" I asked, as I folded my arms over my chest.

"He's hustling, Stephanie," Stanley interjected from the passenger seat, grinning like a carefree child, oblivious to the pitfalls of Tony's lifestyle.

"I was recruited by a new crew, more ruthless than the other one, and now I'm making a ton of money." He reached into his pocket and flashed his drug money in my face.

I wasn't pleased with the path Tony was headed down, but my brother was stubborn, so the most I could do was pray for him every chance I got.

"Tony, you have to be careful. There are people out here who will kill for that money you're flaunting," I said.

He smirked. "I'm not worried about those haters." After darting a furtive glance around, he winked and lifted the front of his shirt, revealing a pistol.

I was speechless. The danger that lingered in the streets warranted him carrying a gun, and I felt overwhelmed by the possibility of him getting hurt or losing his life. But my brother had evolved from hustling for sneaker money to almost achieving kingpin status overnight. An image from my dream flashed through my head: my brother, after the shots were fired. After he was gone. The vision was so intense, so real, that I just stood in silence for a few seconds, absorbing the sight of him before me, alive and well. I did not want to see my brother dead or in jail, but I had a feeling that the consequences of the street life would manifest themselves really soon.

"Are you going to get in or stand there, stuck on stupid?"

The words snapped me out of my ruminations. I wasn't happy with the decisions Tony was making, but I also understood his need to make money and take care of Stanley. For a high school dropout, there weren't many options available. Unfortunately, many of the kids his age sold dope.

"I'm going to get in, Tony, but maybe you could promise me that you will get out of the drug business before you end up in trouble," I said. I tried to instill a lighthearted banter because our little brother was present.

Tony didn't even bother to answer me; he just looked at me like I had two heads, so I equated his silence with a refusal to stop selling. He won this time, but hopefully, this wouldn't be the last time I would plead with him to change his way of life.

Chapter 15

Tony took me and Stanley out to lunch at Mamma Lombardi's; they have the best Italian food in Long Island. It had been a long time since the three of us had been alone together; I enjoyed those moments, talking about school, friends, and our future.

After a while, Stanley left to go to the restroom. As soon as he was out of earshot, Tony told me that he was planning on moving out of our mother's house soon, too, because things there were becoming progressively worse. He didn't actually define *things*, and I didn't ask. He admitted that, in the beginning, he used to give my mother drugs behind my back, just to keep her off the streets, before her drug of choice switched to heroin.

What could I say to that? How could I really judge him when he had just been trying to choose the lesser of two evils?

Then Tony explained that he couldn't take Stanley with him. Because of his lifestyle, he was constantly looking over his shoulder. It would be too dangerous for Stanley to live that sort of life; plus, Tony would feel awful if something happened to his little brother on account of his own actions.

The irony, of course, was the fact that it was too dangerous for Stanley to live in his current situation, anyway.

"So how is your new place, Stephanie?" my brother asked, as Stanley sat back down.

That face flashed in front of my eyes again. *Are you ready?* "It's a lot better than living at home." I cringed at the accidental insult to my brothers. "Except for the fact that I miss you guys so much, I mean."

"We miss you, too, but we understand you had to get out of there," Stanley said with all the maturity of a man three times his age.

I smiled my thanks and changed the subject before I got teary-eyed. "How's school going, Stanley? You are getting straight A's?"

"I'm doing decent," he replied, stealing a glance out the window.

"Are you lying to me, Stanley?" Of course, my tone communicated the fact that I already knew he was full of crap.

He fumbled in his pocket and pulled out his phone. "Sorry, but I really need to answer this. I've been waiting for this call."

Before I could question him further, Tony said, "Go ahead. Take your time."

Then I knew we had more to talk about. I waited patiently while Tony played with his food, long after Stanley had walked away. Finally, speaking so softly that I had to lean forward to hear him, he said, "Listen, I didn't want to say this in front of Stanley, but word on the street is some fellas from a rival crew have it out for me. So I'm just giving you a heads-up." He spoke as if it was no big deal, as if there wasn't a possibility of this news leading to death.

Those were the words that I had feared the most, ever since he'd started hustling in the streets.

"Tony, you can't seriously plan to stay with these guys. You need to stop what you're doing now, before you get hurt." I stared him down, pleading with my eyes.

"It's not that easy, Stephanie. I told you, I'm working for a ruthless group of people; I can't just walk away." His hands swayed from left to right for emphasis.

"Plus, I know too much about this organization for them to allow me to cut ties. They would try to kill me first." He looked directly in my eyes with an unwavering stare that he did not break until Stanley returned.

"You guys look like you're having a serious conversation," Stanley said as his eyes shifted from me to Tony. "What's wrong?"

"Everything is fine," Tony lied, and then he looked in my direction. "Right, Stephanie?"

I didn't speak; I just nodded my head in agreement.

Chapter 16

The theme of Nancy's birthday party was debauchery; we all partied with the intent of making that night one to remember. Nancy's newest boyfriend, Jason, gave her a Prada bag and a gorgeous heart-shaped diamond pendant. In addition to the expensive gifts, he had an open bar, a DJ, and catering available. I sensed that he really cared for Nancy; just by the way he looked at her.

I was having a rough time at the beginning of the party. Debauchery? Seriously? I wish I could have gone home and curled up with *To Kill a Mockingbird*. I had just started the Harper Lee novel a couple of days ago. But Nancy had been so good to me; I couldn't insult her like that. Thank god they had alcohol at this party. I was going to need plenty.

One particular guy was keeping his eyes on me. He followed me around that night and asked for my phone number. I didn't want to give it to him, so I lied and said that I had a boyfriend. That only deterred him the first time. By the third time he approached me, the effect of the alcohol had started to kick in. He no longer looked unattractive; now, he was easy on the eyes.

"Can I help you?" I asked playfully when he tapped me on the shoulder.

"Hey, relax, baby. I just want to talk with you," he said, holding up his hands in surrender.

"Don't call me *baby*." I put my hand on my hip and smiled flirtatiously.

"Feisty. I like feisty." He rubbed his hands together, seemingly in anticipation. "My name is Kevin, and yours?" he asked with a delivery that made me think he had done this over a hundred times before.

"Stephanie." My smile grew broad enough to see from a few blocks away.

"Nice name. I love your smile."

I took a large sip of my drink. I was already pretty inebriated, but every little bit helped.

"So, are you having fun?" he asked.

"Yes." Before this went any further, I had to know the truth. Out of the blue, I demanded, "Are you a womanizer?"

His eyes widened. "No!"

"Oh. Well, that's too bad because I like me a player," I said. I was totally wasted.

"Well, in that case, I might as well come clean." He smiled, then we both laughed at my lighthearted joke and his wittiness.

He offered to get me another drink. I hadn't even realized that I'd finished mine, but sure enough, the cup was empty.

I watched him walk to the bar. He spoke to Nancy for a moment, then she handed him a drink, looked over in my direction, and smiled. Kevin returned a few minutes later and put his arm around me. I didn't pull away.

After a few sips, I started to feel light-headed. "What's in this drink?" I asked him.

"Does it matter?"

The rest of the night was a blank. The next morning, I woke up on the sofa in Nancy's living room, completely nude.

Chapter 17

Two months later, the novelty of being a guest in Nancy's house proved to wear thin. The hospitable disposition that she'd once displayed had been short-lived, and her true colors began to surface. I woke up one morning, surprised when I did not smell anything cooking.

"No breakfast this morning?" I asked as I walked into the kitchen, rubbing my stomach in anticipation of a nice hot meal.

"Running a little behind," Emily explained.

I frowned. On a Sunday morning? They didn't seem especially frantic.

"Bitch, you have to get up and find a job." Nancy put down the morning paper and folded her arms across her chest with all the mannerisms of a parent reprimanding her child.

We were both high-spirited individuals. Often we bantered back and forth, engaging in lighthearted exchanges. If one of us said something that was generally considered derogatory, we would usually smile or laugh so the other person knew that it was all spoken in fun.

That morning, Nancy was dead serious.

"What is your problem?" I asked as gently as possible.

"You're my problem. You barely go to school anymore and you sit around here all day, doing nothing. I'm sick of it!" she shouted.

"Nancy!" Emily reprimanded.

"It's true!" she retorted.

Emily sent me an apologetic glance.

There was a nicer way to address this matter, but Nancy was right; my attendance in school was deplorable. Ever since Mr. Philips had tried pushing up on me, I'd started skipping school for days at a time. I gradually lost interest in my classes, and I was quickly losing a grip on my life.

Instead of holding on to my anger, I realized that Nancy was justified in her reaction. Right then and there, I had an epiphany: it was time to get a job.

"Do you know of anywhere that's hiring?"

Nancy glanced at her sister before she responded. "Well, you're no toothpick anymore. You do have a lot of junk in your trunk, and the gentlemen's club that I work at is always looking for fresh meat." She grinned.

I couldn't believe that, out of all the possible options available, she was encouraging me to become a stripper. And I was still underage! I always thought she had been looking out for my best interests. A few nights ago, Emily told me that Nancy had given Kevin GHB to slip in my drink at her birthday party to loosen me up. Even then, I'd made excuses, thinking that, in her own twisted way, she'd been trying to help me. I had been so wrong about Nancy. Clearly, she was not looking out for my welfare.

Chapter 18

After less than a month at the gentlemen's club, I was making enemies, primarily because the majority of the men were showing up just to watch me dance. I was earning twice as much money as other girls who had been there for years, including Nancy. I was rich. The money was great; I was able to send money to Stanley, so he was doing better than ever. But the way I was earning the cash…the things I had to do…the way those monsters looked at me…. I started to dabble in cocaine, which helped to cloud my judgment and remove my anxiety. Without giving it much thought, I decided to drop out of school during my junior year and devote all of my time to stripping.

I moved out of Nancy's place and got a one-bedroom apartment in a quiet section of Long Island, because she had wanted to charge me a disproportionate amount of money to sleep on her sofa once I started making decent cash. I was a completely different person than I had been a few months ago. I began living a nocturnal life, and I loved it!

I started to have sex with random strangers from the club—for the right fee, of course. It may have seemed strange, considering what I'd been through, but suddenly, I was in charge. I wasn't being forced; I was choosing and getting paid handsomely. It was such a rush!

And it really was fairly easy to do while I was in a drug-induced state, since most of my experiences were a bit blurry. In fact, being high helped to numb any psychological issues that might have erupted from being raped and abused. Once I had drugs in my bloodstream, I could do the most degrading sex acts, things I would never normally engage in if I was sober. I even let this one guy give me a golden shower. He made me a generous offer, and I thought it was worth sacrificing my dignity to buy Stanley new school clothes—that boy was shooting up like a basketball player!

Of course, the money I was earning caused other women to despise me. I even heard rumors of women wanting to cause me bodily harm. Threats didn't deter me, though, because my only concern was making money. Everything else was secondary, including my health. When I was high, I didn't worry about the consequences of having unprotected sex and doing drugs.

I didn't worry about anything.

Chapter 19

One gentleman in particular always came to the club to watch me dance. He showed interest in only me, despite the fact that the veteran dancers were practically tripping over themselves to get his attention. Whenever he walked through the doors, he searched the room. As soon as he spotted me, he was transfixed. The women told me he was a bad apple; they advised me to steer clear of him. But whenever I asked for details, they offered vague responses: "Just trust me on this" or "You don't want to know." To be honest, even if they had told me, I probably would not have listened, anyway. I was getting all of the attention and money now; I was untouchable, and they were jealous. I was sure that, if they'd been in my shoes, they would have taken all the offers, as well.

One night, my biggest fan approached me when I was taking a smoke break outside the club. Maybe he had finally decided to take his fantasy a step further.

"Hey, sweetheart," he said.

I have to admit, he was very dapper in appearance, displaying elegance with a fancy suit and a fresh haircut—just the way I liked my men.

"Hey, yourself," I responded, blowing smoke into his face.

"How would you like to make some extra money tonight?" He gazed intently at my exposed cleavage, then looked up at me and flashed a smile.

"Excuse me?" Of course, I was just pretending that I hadn't heard him; I didn't want to seem desperate. At the time, I thought my reaction was pretty good.

He slipped the cigarette out from between my fingers, took a drag, and blew it in my face. "How would you like to come to my place and give me a private dance?" His eyes were riveted on my breasts.

"You need to set up an appointment, because my schedule is hectic." If I decided to go with him, he would make it worth my time financially.

He laughed at my response. "I got money to blow tonight. Come alone and dance for me and my lonely Maltese," he said, revealing a perfect, seemingly harmless smile.

"You have a Maltese! I love those dogs."

"So, is that a *yes*?" he asked.

Those warnings drifted through my mind. "It's just you and your dog, right?" I asked.

He hesitated, but only for a moment. Then he gave me a disarming smile. "Would I lie to you? Let's go." He walked away without looking back.

I followed him into the night.

Chapter 20

When I got to his place, I should have turned around and walked back out. His living room was full of men sitting around and smoking dope.

No matter how high I was, I knew this was synonymous with trouble. "You said we were going to be alone," I whispered so only he could hear me.

"Don't mind them, sweetheart. I forgot they were going to be here," he said with not an ounce of sincerity.

A tall, slim man with a baseball cap stood up. "Who's the freak bitch?" he shouted, grabbing his crotch. He stalked toward me.

"Watch your mouth, bastard!" I shouted. Oh god, I sounded so pathetic that the other men started to laugh.

"Hurry up and suck his dick, so you can blow us, bitch," Slim demanded.

I turned to...shit; I didn't even know my guy's name. "Are you going to let him speak to me like that?" I asked him.

"He's just playing; don't pay him no mind," he said. Then he grabbed my wrist and pulled me into a bedroom.

Cocaine and vodka were conveniently displayed on the small dresser near the king-size bed. The cocaine was lined up on a small mirror, accompanied by a razor.

He lounged on the bed and gestured grandly. "Make yourself comfortable. Have whatever you want."

After a few lines of cocaine, I had no inhibitions. I could fuck them all.

The man stood up and dropped his pants. I got on my knees and sucked on his manhood until semen rushed out. My technique for giving oral sex had become exceptional; in less than ten minutes, he had ejaculated inside my mouth. He pulled his pants up and walked out of the room, without a word.

Then another man walked in. One at a time, I serviced all of the men from the living room. The guy from the strip club came back in and paid generously for my services. I began getting dressed, then someone from the living room shouted that there was one more man, a late arrival.

I shook my head. "No way. I've already been paid."

"Right." He dazzled me with his smile. "A girl has to have her priorities." He pulled a twenty out of his wallet, then walked out.

I quickly got stationed on my knees, ready to give head one more time.

As I waited, I realized that I hadn't exchanged names with a single man, including the one who had just paid me. I shrugged. As long as their money was green, names were irrelevant.

The door opened.

I was as good as dead.

"Stephanie, what the fuck are you doing?"

I was speechless. I'd never seen Tony look so cold.

Then he was across the room, punching me in the face.

Thankfully, everything went pitch black.

Chapter 21

So much happened over the next year. Tony beat me up that night, so bad that I was hospitalized for two weeks. That was the last time I saw him alive—yelling at me, filled with fury. Shortly after, he was gunned down by a rival gang member. The memorial service for Tony was packed; the only person missing was my dope fiend mother.

After Tony died, Stanley's grandmother on his father's side sent for him. She had been living alone in Brooklyn for years, ever since her husband died. Our mother was still so negligent; she probably wouldn't even notice Stanley's absence—at least, not until she needed something. She was showing no signs of kicking her habit.

Stanley came to my apartment to say goodbye. He found me unconscious, with a syringe in my arm.

The knowledge that Tony's last thought of me had been one of rage and disgust led me to attempt suicide. Obviously, I failed. Stanley found me and called 911. Stanley didn't just save my life that day. He saved my life forever. He's the reason I finally decided to get my life in order.

For starters, I began attending therapy sessions twice a week. I was slowly learning to confront my past and to contemplate my future. I stopped working at the gentlemen's club, because that wasn't the image I wanted to portray. I started going to church, and I got a respectable 9-to-5 job as a home health aide. I also got my GED, which made me feel—somewhat—like a productive individual in society. During my GED course, I established some friendly and healthy relationships with several people.

I became close with one guy in particular. David was tall and handsome, with an athletic build. He definitely had sex appeal, but more importantly, he was such a charming man. Whenever I was with him, I had the overwhelming feeling that I had met him before; somehow, his eyes seemed so familiar to me. I had bumped into him at his uncle's church during Sunday service one morning, and David and I started building a relationship from there.

Surprisingly, we had a lot in common: we both were family-oriented, and we were horror-movie fanatics. David was even an avid reader, like me. Obviously, our faith was also another common factor. He attended services with me every other week, because his father was the pastor at another church, so David alternated between the two. He sang in the church choir. His voice was so beautiful and filled with such gusto that just hearing it aroused me.

We had been dating for a few months when David called me one Sunday and changed my life.

"I missed hearing you sing in church today," I told him. "You're amazing."

"Thank you. I think you are amazing, too."

I laughed. "What are you talking about? I can't sing!"

"Who said anything about singing? You are just amazing."

For just a moment, we savored the moment in silence.

"Where do you see yourself five years from now?" he suddenly asked.

I smiled as I pictured my future. "I see myself as a mother, married to a handsome man, who is articulate and assertive. I see myself happy."

"That sounds awesome," he said.

It sure did. "How about you? Where do you see yourself in five years?" I asked.

"I see myself married to you. And I see everything you just said."

At first, I was confused. Did he just say what I thought he said?

"Hello? You still there?" he asked.

"Oh, sorry! Yes, I-I'm still here," I stuttered like a fool.

"Are you okay?" he asked. "Was it something I said?"

I sighed. "Yes, David, it was something you said. When you propose to me, it will be a dream come true."

Chapter 22

A month later, I asked to leave work early because I was feeling nauseous. Everything I ate, I threw up. I thought I might be pregnant, so I called David. As soon as he heard what was happening, he told me he'd pick up a pregnancy test and be right over. I curled up in bed and waited.

I felt bad, because I was supposed to visit Emily that afternoon. Recently, Nancy had been killed as the result of a date rape; her killer was still at large. Emily couldn't deal with her grief. She attempted suicide, which landed her in a mental institution. Hopefully, she would get released soon. For the moment, though, she was where she needed to be.

She had been so happy for me during our last visit, when I'd described David to her.

I suddenly heard my front door open, then I heard his familiar footsteps.

"Babe, I'm here. Are you okay?" David knelt beside the bed. He wasn't like any other guy I'd ever met. Based on his attentiveness to me, I knew he would make a good father.

"I feel horrible, babe. I just want to take this test and see what's going on," I said, as he helped me to my feet.

He stopped me from moving past him and looked into my eyes. "Do you want to be pregnant?" His tone had shifted from concerned to serious.

Truth be told, I wanted the results to be negative because I considered myself a traditional girl; I wanted to get married before I started my own family. But I had a feeling that he wanted me to be pregnant, so I said what he wanted to hear; I didn't want to upset him.

"Yes, baby," I said, as I forced a smile to stretch across my face.

He studied me, as if gauging my level of truthfulness. "Same here, so let's keep our fingers crossed," he said after a moment, reciprocating with a smile.

My fingers were crossed, but secretly, for the opposite reason. He held my hand as we walked inside the bathroom.

After a couple of minutes, he jumped up and carefully spun me around the cramped room. According to the test, we were expecting a child.

Chapter 23

David was finally taking me to meet his parents. I had a feeling that he was going to propose. I had already hinted to him that marriage would be our next logical step. I reminded him how important it was for me to do things traditionally, partly because I had never had many traditions growing up. I was so excited to meet his parents and begin this new phase of my life; there was nothing in the world that could possibly put a damper on my mood. I'd heard so much about his family. I felt like I already knew them. David didn't have any siblings. His mother was a nurse, and his father was a revered pastor in the community. David was very close to his father; he told me that his dad was a philanthropist with an immense heart. In his spare time, the man helped the homeless, as well as battered women and children. What a difference between our families!

David hadn't told his parents about the baby yet. I was only one month along, so we had some time. But he had told them our relationship was serious, which was why they'd invited me over. They were traditional people.

David was overwhelmed with excitement, but I was so nervous—I couldn't stop biting my nails. As we walked up the driveway, I was visibly shaking. Then David rang the doorbell, and an older lady opened the door and smiled.

"David! Nice of you to make it, honey."

He kissed his mother on the cheek and gave her a hug.

She shifted her attention toward me. "You must be Stephanie."

"Hi. Nice to finally meet you," I said.

"Same here. Come inside and meet my lovely husband," she said.

A broad smile on my face, I walked into the living room. David's father was sitting on the sofa, still in his preaching attire from Sunday service. He quickly stood up to formally greet me.

My smile vanished. My mouth opened on a silent scream.

David's father was the man who had first raped me.

Stephanie's Diary

Part 2

Chapter 24

The last thing I remember was feeling dizzy as the room began spinning out of control. Then my legs gave out; I felt like someone had pulled the rug from underneath me. On my way down, my head crashed into something; then I blacked out. I could not see anything, but I could hear everything. I was unconscious.

"Oh my God, Stephanie, are you all right?" Victoria screamed.

What? Was she kidding? Did I look all right?

"Gary, honey call an ambulance," she said.

He seemed slow on the uptake. "O-okay, dear," Gary said.

David got down on the floor and cradled me in his arms.

"Stephanie, please wake up," he cried.

He was an emotional wreck; I could even feel his tears rain down on my face.

Please, don't cry, my love.

* * * * *

There weren't enough words to describe my rage when I found out my boyfriend's father was the man who'd raped me. The thoughts that I entertained were cruel and malicious. I had a craving for blood, and nothing would get in my way. I promised myself that, as soon as I was able to walk again, he would be a dead man.

I was in a coma for what felt like an eternity. Sometimes I was sure that I would never get another opportunity to open my eyes. It was a scary thought, one that I considered way too often. This was probably almost as bad as being buried alive.

Stanley came to visit me in the hospital today. Hearing his voice kept me sane. He walked in and greeted me with the usual kiss on the forehead. But this time it felt different—it had more emotion attached to it.

I heard him pull up a chair to the edge of my bed so he was sitting close to me, just like he normally did during his visits.

"Stephanie, I miss you so much."

He seemed to be in a somber mood. He grabbed my hand, and I could feel his warm touch; it made me feel alive. He kissed my hand, held it gently, then continued to speak.

"I'm sorry to be the bearer of bad news, but I have to tell you this."

He was sniffling as he spoke, and although I could not see him, I could picture tears rolling down his handsome face. I wanted to tell him not to cry. I wished I could do something to make him feel better.

"Stephanie. We're alone." He paused. I heard him take a deep breath. "Last night, our next door neighbor, Mark, said his dog led him to our mother's house. Mark got suspicious when he saw the door ajar. He stepped inside and saw our mother sprawled out on the living room floor, unconscious. He called the cops, and the ambulance came, but it was too late. She died from a heroin overdose. You'll never believe this, but I spoke to her a week ago, and she told me that she'd failed us as a parent. She wanted me to tell you she was sorry for everything."

Pain lanced through my chest at his words. This was awful. My mother and I weren't close anymore, but I still loved her. And I'd hoped that she would get clean. But now she was gone. I wanted to cry, but the tears would not surface. My brother needed me, now more than ever. I could hear it in his voice.

"What am I to do now, Stephanie?"

I tried so badly to speak, but those comforting words could not find a way out of my mouth.

"I never met my father. Tony is dead, and now Mom, too. Stephanie, what will I do if I lose you next?"

I hated to hear my little brother grieving. This was too much for me to deal with. I continued to fight to free my voice, but I got the same heartbreaking results. Nothing.

"Stephanie, please, say something! You've been in a coma for a month, and they're talking about pulling the plug soon. Don't do this to me! I need you."

Stanley started sobbing uncontrollably, and I felt tears start to well up in my eyes. Then, finally, my tears started to flow, and my eyes opened.

"Stanley, I'm here for you."

"Stephanie, you're awake!"

He was screaming so loud, several staff members came rushing into the room. When they realized what had happened, broad smiles spread across their faces, and cheers echoed off the walls.

* * * * *

When I got out of the hospital, I had trouble getting back into the swing of things. My life once again shifted gears; I could not catch a break for nothing. I was issued another emotional scar; unfortunately, due to complications, I had miscarried while in the hospital. For months, I was consumed by depression. I even contemplated getting high, because I could not bear the pain of being sober. When I thought of how far I had come, though, I decided against the idea. I returned to therapy to try and regain stability in my life. David was there for me every step of the way. Stanley and I called each other daily. A few times, I heard raucous sounds in the background. I overheard snippets of conversation referring to random acts of violence and a confrontation over someone's turf. I hoped he wasn't headed down the wrong path. When I asked him about it, he denied doing anything wrong, and he said I was hearing things. Some things never change: I still knew when my little brother was being dishonest with me. But all I could do was pray for him and ask God to watch over him, because he was the only family I had left.

Chapter 25

March 18, 2004

The mental institution looked dismal. The building was not adorned with many windows, and it was located near an ominous wooded area. Once inside, it was sometimes difficult to tell the staff from the patients, because the staff walked around like zombies.

When I went to see Emily, the supervisor told me that she was in a new location in the building because she had tried to escape recently. Her condition had gotten worse; she was becoming delusional.

When Emily finally came out to the visiting room, I almost did not recognize her. She had a deranged look in her eyes that sent chills up my spine. I agreed with the supervisor: she seemed to have gotten worse.

"Emily, is that you?" I asked.

Her eyes were wide, and she kept looking over her shoulder and mumbling incoherently to herself. Paranoia.

"Hey, Stephanie. Long time, *no see*. Is everything okay?"

Without going into detail, I told her that I had suffered a small accident. I didn't want to worry her; she seemed to be going through enough.

"An accident?" Her eyes got even wider.

What she said next further confirmed the fact that the young lady I had once called my best friend was no longer.

"Stephanie, did the aliens abduct you, too?"

"What are you talking about?" I asked.

"I saw them. They abducted me. I even got to see the inside of their spaceship, but they let me go for some reason."

I was at a loss for words. She was speaking so fast. Was I hearing her right?

"Emily, slow down and take a deep breath."

She hung her head. "You don't believe me, either."

She sounded disappointed. I didn't want to upset her. "No. I believe you, Emily."

"In my old room at this place, when I used to look out the window, I would see their spaceship late at night," she said.

I shook my head. Emily would not stop talking about being abducted by aliens. It hurt me to see my best friend lose her grip on reality.

Just then, my phone rang. A glance at the screen showed me that David's mother, Victoria, was calling. "Hello," I answered in the middle of Emily's description of the spaceship.

Emily slammed her palms onto the table. "Is that them? Is that the aliens?"

I leapt to my feet and hurried to the corner of the room, cupping my hand over the mouthpiece.

"Excuse me?" Victoria demanded.

"Sorry about that. Is everything all right?"

"That depends," she sighed. "My friend's son is turning ten, and I need to bake two hundred cupcakes for his birthday party! Gary can't help because he's away on a new business venture, and David is working late…"

"Stephanie! Hang up on them! They can zap you through the phone!"

I turned and glared at Emily. "I'll see you tonight," I told Victoria.

Chapter 26

I'd first met my friend, Debra, during my GED class. Afterward, she was very supportive to me in the hospital; not a week went past that she did not visit me. I was so glad to spend time with her again, out of a hospital room!

Debra was beautiful, but she did not take pride in her appearance. She didn't wear any make-up, and she always wore her hair shoved into a ponytail that looked like it hadn't been touched for days. She was self-conscious about her butt, so she always hid it; this time, she had a red sweater wrapped around her waist.

We walked past an astrology shop on Main Street in Patchogue, and she thought it would be a good idea to check the place out. She said that people had told her the place gave pretty accurate tarot readings.

I was not so sure about it, but I finally gave in after she promised to take me out to lunch at a Thai restaurant down the street called Lawan. I couldn't say no to sushi.

When we walked into the shop, though, the image of the death card flashed in my mind. The hair stood up on the back of my neck. I had dealt with enough death already. Oh, God, don't let Stanley be next. I would lose my mind!

Debra noticed my hesitation and grabbed my wrist. "Don't be a big baby," she teased, as she tugged on my arm.

"I'm not being a baby; I just don't know if this is such a good idea."

"It's a good idea—trust me."

There was nobody in sight, and yet I could feel a presence, as if someone were in the room with us. It was starting to feel like a scene out of a horror movie. I had a feeling this would not end so well.

"There's nobody here. Let's go," I said.

We turned toward the exit, and we both screamed. Standing in front of us was a short old lady with loose skin and long grey hair trailing down her back. She looked at least one hundred years of age.

"I'm sorry to startle you," she said.

"Hey! What's your problem? You scared the hell out of us!" Debra shouted.

"I'm truly sorry, but I didn't mean to," the old lady said.

Debra took a deep breath. "Well, don't worry about it. My friend and I would like a reading, please," she said.

"Of course. Right this way." She pointed toward a small table with a deck of tarot cards placed in the center.

"So, who wants to go first?" she asked.

I was scared. And I was starting to think that Debra was scared, too. Neither one of us jumped at the invitation. We both stood there, silent, then Debra cleared her throat.

"She will go first."

I rolled my eyes, then took a seat.

As soon as I told the woman my name, I began to sweat—not because it was hot, but because I was nervous.

"Relax, dear." The lady extended her wrinkled hand for me to grab.

69

Debra gave me a pat on the shoulder. "It will be fun!"

I scowled at her. Too little, too late.

"What would you like to know?" the woman asked.

I took a moment to think about what mattered most. "What direction is my life headed in? What about my health? Will I ever be able to leave my past behind?"

The old woman closed her eyes for a moment, then removed several cards from the deck.

"The first card is the devil card, and it implies indulgence, addiction, and something else that you indulge in that feels good, but is not good for your health or well-being."

I remained silent, waiting for her to elaborate.

"In your past, did you indulge in drugs?" she asked.

"Yeah. That was a good guess," I said.

She didn't find humor in my remark. "I don't make these things up, honey," she said. Then she drew a second card. "Three of swords. This card indicates some type of difficult loss."

Her blue eyes bore into me, as if looking into my soul. "I see you were hurt when your brother passed, because when he died, you two weren't on good terms."

I nodded my head in disbelief. How was she so good? I never expected such accuracy.

"You suffered a loss while in the hospital, too, but this hurt was not as deep."

She then reached for another card. "Nine of swords. This card pertains to mental torment, insomnia, and depression."

I sat there, thinking of how I had been finding it hard to sleep lately, because of the memories from my troubled past.

One last card.

She reached for the deck.

It was the death card.

It was the card I had feared the most. Instantly, I began crying. After I regained my composure, she told me that my car would be tampered with by someone involved in trafficking of some sort.

She also told me that danger was imminent and that I should stay clear of basements in the near future. When I asked her to elaborate, she just repeated her warning: stay away from basements in the near future.

That's when Debra had a sudden change of heart. She didn't want a reading. But she still bought me lunch.

Chapter 27

Before I even opened my car door, I called Victoria and told her I'd be a little late—then I spent at least ten minutes promising her that I wasn't bailing, and that I would really show up and help her with the baking. I didn't know much about cars, so I made a quick call to my brother. Following his advice, I drove to Bellport, and pulled into Eastern Automotive on Station Road. Somehow, Stanley had connections. A man named Teddy introduced himself right away, and didn't blink an eye when I explained that I wanted my car checked for any type of tampering. Teddy and his staff went right to work, even though there were other customers waiting. Within a half hour, he assured me that the car was in good working condition and it had not been tampered with. I felt a little silly after all was said and done, but it was a monumental relief to know that the voodoo lady was just another nutcase trying to make a buck.

* * * * *

By the time I arrived at David's parents' house, Victoria had almost finished with the baking. But there were still two hundred cupcakes to frost. After we finished, we decided to make one of my favorite meals, sausage and peppers. While dicing up peppers and onions, I tried to make small talk.

"What type of business is Gary away on?"

She blinks in surprise. "He wants to keep it under the radar until the time is right," she said.

That was weird. When I had asked David, he had given me the same response. Now I really wanted to know what activities Gary was into. Why was everyone being so secretive?

"Can you give me a hint?" I asked.

She acted like she hadn't heard me and changed the subject. But I planned on mentioning it again later.

"My son is a lucky man," she said.

"Why do you say that?" I asked.

"Because he has you in his life, silly." She smiled and winked at me.

I hesitantly returned the smile. "Thank you, Victoria."

"Call me Mom."

I was surprised by the offer. Not long after leaving the hospital, I had told her about my relationship with my mother. Maybe she felt sorry for me and wanted to play surrogate mom. I savored the moment.

"I'm really sorry about the baby," she said.

I didn't quite know how to respond to that, so I just sat there and took a deep breath before speaking. "We will work on having another baby when the time is right," I said.

All of a sudden, her eyes started twitching and her face scrunched up in palpable anger.

"When the time is right? What's wrong with right now? Are you saying my David isn't good enough for you?"

I was bombarded with questions; she didn't even give me a chance to answer the initial one! She had done a complete turnaround.

"No, not at all; that's not what I was trying to say!"

"Then what are you trying to say?" Veronica stopped cutting peppers and slammed the knife on the counter. Her eyes flared.

I wanted to be careful about the way I answered her because there was a butcher knife on the counter, and I had seen her glance at it. I was so frightened that I began stammering. "I-I didn't mean to-to offend you, Mom."

"You can call me Victoria," she snarled.

I had definitely hit a nerve. I didn't want to make the situation any worse, so I kept quiet and allowed her to vent.

Her voice rose as she continued her tirade. "I really liked you. For a minute, you had me fooled; I thought you were different from any other girl David had introduced us to. But I guess I was wrong."

"I'm so sorry if I offended you." I only hoped she could see the true remorse in my eyes.

"You didn't just offend me." She pointed to herself. "You offended my family as well."

"What do you mean?" I stared at her, utterly confused.

She ignored my question. "David and his father listen to me. If I tell them that you're not good for our family, they will listen to me."

"Please, don't do that," I pleaded.

"Give me one good reason why I shouldn't!"

"Because I love him."

She waved her hand in dismissal.

"Not like me and my husband do," she said.

And then she got quiet, rolled her eyes, and excused herself. If I had to guess, I would assume dinner was being cancelled. I was ready to leave, anyway.

I thought I heard her on the phone, but I could not make out what she was saying. When she came back into the kitchen, she was not as cordial as she had initially been, but at least her head wasn't doing a 360. To my surprise, we finished preparing dinner and then set the table. I waited to eat until Victoria had tried the food first. Secure in the knowledge that she hadn't tried to poison me, I was able to relax a bit, and actually enjoy the meal. While we were eating, I thought I heard the front door open and close. When I mentioned it, however, Victoria dismissed my concern by telling me I was hearing things. I was hearing that response a lot lately. In fact, I was starting to understand how Emily must feel!

After supper was over and I'd helped with the dishes, Victoria suggested that we have ice cream and watch television, but I declined. It was getting late, and I wanted to leave before David's father came home. Every time I mentioned leaving, though, Victoria tried to get me to stay a little longer.

"When is David's father coming back home?"

"He should be here soon."

That was all I needed to hear.

"Victoria, it was nice spending time with you, but I really should be going."

"Why so soon?"

"I have to be up early in the morning for a job interview."

Her eyes narrowed. "What time is your interview?" she asked.

I thought quickly. "It's at ten o'clock."

"Okay, honey, then you do need to get going. I'm sorry for my attitude earlier, but I'm just overprotective when it comes to my family."

"I understand."

"We have to do this again sometime."

Yeah, right. This would never happen again.

When I got up to leave, I did not see my car keys near my purse where I had left them. I knew I wasn't losing my mind, so I asked Victoria if she had seen them. She claimed ignorance. After a half hour of searching for my keys in the living room, kitchen, and even the bathroom, I still could not find them. I was getting frustrated, because I knew that I had placed my purse and car keys on the table near the front door.

Then I heard the front door open and close.

"Honey, I'm home."

This was what I had been trying to avoid. Now Gary was here, and I had to leave before I went into a rage and his blood was on my hands.

"Something sure does smell good," he said, as he walked into the living room and gave his wife a kiss on the forehead. He looked at me with his large brown eyes and grinned.

"Thanks honey. Stephanie and I cooked dinner. She was just asking about you."

"Is that right?" he said, while rubbing his chin.

"I was just leaving, but I can't find my keys," I coldly explained.

That's when he reached in his pants pocket and handed me a set of keys.

"I found these in the driveway. Do they look familiar?"

"Those are my keys. That's strange."

He handed them to me. I had to hold back the urge to snatch them from his grasp. Instead, I took them calmly and ground out my thanks. I don't know how my keys got outside, but I know I brought them inside with me and placed them near my purse. I would worry about it later; at the moment, I just wanted to leave. I gave Victoria a hug and a peck on the cheek, and then headed out the door.

Inside my car, I had a flashback, which resulted in a panic attack. At long last, I took a deep breath. I put the key inside the ignition, but my car wouldn't start. I tried again. I got the same result. I had just gotten a full tank of gas, so I knew that could not have been the issue. As I pondered my dilemma, I realized that I was sitting on something.

I reached beneath my rear end and came away with a wallet. One I'd never seen. When I opened it, Gary's picture stared at me from the driver's license. That confirmed it: David's father had been inside my car. Now he was going to feel my wrath.

I stormed up to the front door and knocked. I didn't get an answer. I knocked once again, harder this time, and got the same result. Growing impatient, I reached for the door handle and twisted it. It was unlocked. I strode inside, walked into the kitchen, opened a drawer, and grabbed the largest knife I could find. This would be the last time he fucked with me. I was going to make sure of that.

As I walked through the house, I heard Gary's voice.

"I found a buyer."

"That's great, honey."

"He should be here for her soon."

"Are you going to miss her?"

"Maybe a little bit, but I will get another sex slave," Gary said.

A sex slave? Those words brought back the memory of Gary raping me. I wanted to vomit.

"She is so beautiful; I'm going to miss seeing her face," Victoria said.

"The buyer will be here shortly. I will be in the basement if you need me, dear," Gary said.

I heard the doorbell ring; it must be the buyer. I knew that I had to beat him down to the basement. The safety of this "sex slave" was more important than revenge.

I walked down the basement stairs. As soon as I reached the bottom, I noticed a queen-size bed, with an expensive camera positioned on a stand in front of it. I knew right away that pornographic home videos were being made.

Then, my eyes started to tear up. I was looking at a cage. Inside was a young girl, not much older than thirteen or fourteen years old.

She was wearing a sports bra and panties, and she had a collar around her neck, as if she were an animal.

My hands fumbled for the phone in my pocket and my fingers jabbed 911, but since I was in the basement, I didn't have a strong enough signal for service.

I approached the cage, intent on setting her free, but I needed a key to unlock it. Gary had made sure she would not escape.

What type of activity was this preacher into?

The young girl appeared to be drugged, judging by the way she sat there, nodding.

Even though I didn't sense an immediate threat, I still moved with caution.

"Hey, you," I said as loud as I could without being heard upstairs.

She did not respond. The stupor of whatever drug they had her on hadn't worn off yet.

Not wanting to waste any more time, I started searching nearby for the key.

I searched just about every place I could think of, with no success. Maybe Gary had the keys on him. If I couldn't free her at the moment, I'd just have to bring help back with me.

Then I heard the door open. I knew I didn't have much time to go into hiding.

"I have to find a place to hide; I will be right back," I told the girl, even though she was still too heavily medicated to respond.

No one had come down the stairs, yet I suddenly heard another voice in the basement.

"I have to find a place to hide; I will be right back," the voice mocked me.

I knew I was in a world of trouble now.

Chapter 28

"I have to find a place to hide; I will be right back." The parrot repeated these words, over and over, until Gary walked over to pacify it.

"Is there someone here?" the other man asked, as his blue eyes scanned the basement.

"Don't worry, John. Nobody is here but me, you, and my sex slave," Gary responded.

"I hope so," the man said, clearing his throat nervously.

He had every right to be tense; if I had a job working for the postal service—with great benefits, I hear—I would be tense, too. He was still in uniform; his craving must be really intense.

"Don't mind Teresa. My pet parrot is getting old, so she has been repeating things from the past a lot lately."

All of a sudden, the girl in the cage stood up. "There is someone else here," she said.

My heart skipped a beat.

Gary and John got quiet. Both men approached her cage.

"Who is here?" John asked.

"Tell me at once!" Gary shouted.

The girl hesitated before continuing. "She is leaving. Go catch her before she escapes!" She pointed in the direction of the empty staircase, while laughing at the men.

"You think you are funny? You will be punished for that." Gary reached for a whip hanging on the wall. The device seemed to strike fear in the young girl. "I'm sorry! I was only joking!" she cried as she sat on the floor and placed both hands together, interlocking her fingers.

"Too late for that; now, shut your mouth at once!" Gary continued shouting unnecessarily.

I could see everything from my position under the bed. Gary was clearly in complete control of the situation; he was just showing off in front of his guest. I rolled my eyes at his ridiculous antics.

And the girl… So she could talk. I could only hope she wouldn't turn me in.

* * * * *

The negotiation process between the men commenced.

"This one will be of more value because her vagina is much tighter than the last girl I sold to you," Gary said. Both men stood there, literally starting to drool over the exposed young girl. Her scanty clothing didn't leave much to the imagination of the perverse men.

John smiled and wiped saliva from the corners of his mouth. "The last girl I purchased from you was wonderful. She entertained me twice a day, every day, but it wasn't long before I became jaded with her."

"Do you still own her?" Stephanie detected a hint of desperation in Gary's voice.

"No. I sold her to my brother," he said.

"Which brother—the policeman or the school teacher?" Gary asked.

"The policeman."

"I hope you didn't take a loss."

"My brother was a virgin to this sort of entertainment; he was so desperate, I nearly doubled my profit. I sold it to him for five thousand more than what I paid for it."

"Good. You just have to be very careful who you negotiate with." A hint of concern edged into Gary's voice.

"I am. I cover my tracks very well, so you don't have to worry," John said.

"Okay. So are you ready to get down to business?"

"I thought you would never ask." John looked toward the cage, while licking his lips.

Chapter 29

I had to cover my mouth, so the sound of my sobs would not travel. I could not help but think about how many young women were coerced into having sex while the camera was rolling. I reached in my pocket and pulled out my cell phone to dial 911 again, but I still could not get through because of bad reception down in the basement.

"Stand up," Gary ordered the young girl.

"Please. Don't do this to me again," the girl pleaded, as her tears began to drop.

"You will obey me. You know what happened the last time you were disobedient," Gary commented.

"What happened last time?" John asked with the same level of excitement as a kid in a candy store.

"Let's just say that she could not sit properly for quite some time." Gary started laughing uncontrollably.

"Now, stand up at once!" he roared, after regaining his composure.

The girl complied, and I could see streams of tears flowing down her pretty chocolate-hued face. "Please don't do this, mister," she cried.

Her tears of sorrow were ignored, and her pleas for mercy fell on deaf ears. The men were gearing up to have a field day with the young girl. There was nothing I could do to help her because there was no telling what they would do to me if they found me there.

"Please don't do this, mister," Gary mocked. "Save it for someone who cares. Pleading for help will not benefit you. But if you shut up and do what you are told, I might not be as rough this time," he snarled.

Gary walked over to the cage and reached inside his pants pocket for a set of keys. Once he opened the cage, he beckoned for the girl to come to him, but she hesitated.

He yanked her by the chain around her neck, just like he would to a dog. I could see the discomfort on her face, as he handled her as if she were less than human.

"Please, don't do this to me!" she said. She kicked at him wildly. Then she threw a wild jab at Gary and missed.

Out of nowhere, Gary slapped her. Hard. I almost cried out for her. I couldn't stand to watch any more abuse! It was a miracle that the child did not bruise, but she did pass out.

"Now, I will teach you. And you will learn how to listen," he shouted, spittle raining down on her face. Gary reached in his pocket and grabbed a needle and a small glass bottle of clear liquid. He removed the cap from the needle and stuck the tip in the small bottle to retrieve the liquid. I could tell by the dozens of blemishes on the girl's arm that this form of abuse had been occurring for quite some time.

"Her breasts are developing so nicely," John noted, as he put his hand over his crotch in an attempt to cover his bulging erection.

"Believe me when I tell you that I had a lot of good times with this one. For the right price, she can be yours." Gary's voice rang with pride, as if he were bragging about a favorite car.

"Oh, I believe you; she's so hot, she's making me perspire," John said, as he wiped imaginary sweat from his forehead.

Gary then removed the collar. John retreated in surprise at the sight of the unsightly bruises around her neck.

"You need to learn how to control yourself, preacher. I don't want damaged goods," John remarked as he shook his head.

"You're right, and I'm sorry for my exuberance."

Oh, really? He didn't look sorry.

"Since you are a valued customer, I will give you a discount," Gary added.

John's face lit up. There's nothing like a good bargain.

* * * * *

Within ten minutes, John had examined the girl from head to toe—thoroughly—and the men had wrapped the poor girl up in bed linens, in order to smuggle her out of the basement and into John's vehicle undetected. Judging by the way the men worked pleasantly together, I bet that they did this type of thing pretty often. They worked efficiently, without exchanging much dialogue; in fact, each man operated as if he could read the other's mind as they carried the girl up the stairs and out of the basement. After a few minutes, both men came back. Gary picked up a needle and filled it with a clear liquid. Then he nodded his head at John. Like lightning, both men rushed to the bed and pulled me from underneath, then injected the substance into my arm. I tried to put up a fight, but within seconds, I passed out.

When I regained consciousness, I opened my eyes and realized that I was lying on a cold floor and I could barely breathe. I was inside the same cage the young girl had been in. And my neck had the same collar around it.

"Somebody, help me!"

Chapter 30

For the first time in my life, I wished that I was having a nightmare. I tried to free myself from the collar around my neck, even though I knew that it was physically impossible without access to the key. Then I heard the basement door open, followed by footsteps.

"Nice of you to make it here on such short notice," Gary said.

The man he was talking to was Caucasian, with brown tousled hair and a five o'clock shadow.

"Once you told me you had an eighteen-year-old slave with a bubble ass and a tight pussy, I would have been a fool to let the opportunity pass me by," the stranger said.

Gary grinned. "The young ones don't usually last long. My son, David, knows how to pick them."

"Bubble ass and a tight pussy," the parrot mocked.

Both men laughed at the stupid bird. They were perverse, even the bird.

"How is David? I haven't seen him since you sold me the twelve-year-old. He lured her by promising her a puppy, as I recall," the man said.

Gary nodded. "David is fine. Most likely, he's out looking for more prey."

I could not believe my ears. I thought David was my soul mate!

85

And this stranger—he was a savage! However, he did not fit the description of a predator in the slightest way. He was dressed elegantly with a collared shirt and tie, nice slacks, and shined shoes. He even carried the scent of expensive cologne. Everything about him screamed upper crust. Without saying a word, his very body language demanded respect. It wouldn't surprise me at all to find out that he was a kingpin in the sex-trafficking world.

"Here she is, just as I promised." Gary gestured grandly toward the cage—toward me. The bastard.

"She's even more beautiful than I imagined," the man said.

"And she will be your property soon enough."

The white man rubbed his hands together while he gazed hungrily at me. I felt like a piece of meat. Judging from the look in his eyes, I knew he was planning on getting his money's worth.

He gave Gary a briefcase full of crisp bills in exchange for me.

Gary's face lit up. Then he grabbed a needle and filled it with clear liquid to sedate me. I was still feeling lethargic from the last time he'd drugged me, so I didn't put up much resistance this time. I felt a pinch when the needle entered my arm; my eyes were already getting heavy as the drug took effect.

* * * * *

Later, when I opened my eyes, I was no longer in Gary's basement. I hadn't the slightest clue where I was. I was nude, tied to a bed. And the man who'd given Gary the briefcase full of money was standing naked beside me, with an enormous erection. He didn't waste much time. Before I knew it, he was on top of me, sucking on my nipples. He then proceeded to force his manhood inside me; the pain was unbearable.

"Oh God, help me!" I screamed.

He laughed. "Not even God can help you now."

I blacked out.

When I regained consciousness, I was someplace else.

Chapter 31

I was awakened by the feel of something digging into my flesh. I opened my eyes and screamed at the top of my lungs when I saw two huge rats feeding on my left arm. I brushed them away, then stood up to run, but something yanked me back. I fell onto my hands and knees. The huge rodents must have been equally afraid, because I could hear them scampering away in the opposite direction.

The pain in my ankle was excruciating. I was certain that I'd broken something when I had fallen. But I couldn't let that stop me. I mustered all of my strength to stand back up. As I did so, I noticed a thick silver chain attached to my left ankle. That would make it difficult for me to get very far. I brushed my knees off; they were tender to the touch. And when I looked at my hands, I realized that they were bleeding from the fall. I could also feel a sharp, burning sensation on my left arm. I started to cry when I realized the lacerations were actually several hideous bite marks from the rodents.

The cement floor under me was wet, and I could hear what sounded like water dripping from someplace nearby. I looked over to my right and saw a pink hair bow lying there. Beside it was a Barbie doll. I picked it up, then dropped it and shied away from it when I saw that it was adorned with fresh blood. The doll must belong to the twelve-year-old that the men had spoken of briefly.

I heard a door swing open slowly, followed by heavy footsteps.

"Nice to see you're awake," the voice called out. "Are you hungry?"

I nodded my head and was handed a tray of food that resembled vomit. It smelled awful, but I was extremely hungry. I didn't devote much time to critiquing what my meal looked like. I wasn't sure what the food consisted of, but maybe I didn't want to know; whatever it was, it tasted like crap.

My body felt severely parched. After I finished eating, the man handed me a glass of water. If his housekeeping was as bad as the gross look of the glass, he probably didn't get many visitors. The glass had lipstick around the mouth piece. What appeared to be rat droppings were floating on the surface. I hesitated.

The man squatted down and stared at my face until my eyes met his. "Don't act boogie," he snarled.

The last thing I wanted to do was upset him, so I drank from the glass. Instantly I felt nauseous. I could feel the small objects from the glass of water swim around in my mouth as I drank from it. Since my stomach was weak, and it already had all that it could handle, I threw up.

Some of the water landed on the man's boots.

"I'm deeply sorry," I said.

He looked at his boots. He appeared to be an inch away from wrapping his hands around my neck and choking the life out of me. Even though the glass and the water looked unsavory, I decided to finish drinking it to appease him. After I finished off the glass of water, he nodded.

"Listen to me, and you listen clear. You will address me as Vincent, and from here on out, you will not speak unless spoken to." He paused. "You will remain here for a very long time, so I suggest that you get used to it."

"Why are you doing this to me?" I asked.

My question hit a nerve. Vincent stood up and kicked me in the stomach. The blow knocked the wind out of me, but once I caught my breath, my scream filled the basement, and tears of agony rolled down my cheeks. The pain was unbelievable. And he wasn't done. He kicked me several times in my stomach. I begged him to stop, but that only seemed to add fuel to the fire.

It was the first time he beat me. But I had a feeling that it would not be the last.

Chapter 32

First I heard a single shot, followed by shouting and heavy footsteps. Then a thump. The noise over my head traveled in front of the basement door. Then everything went silent. Suddenly, the door opened, and I saw a group of people dressed in black, their faces covered as they strode down the staircase toward me.

These must be Vincent's colleagues. A few days prior, I'd overheard a heated argument about money, and his colleagues had made death threats.

As the group in black got closer, though, I stared in disbelief. My prayers had been answered. Over the years, I'd gradually lost faith in everyone: family, law enforcement, and religion. Now, my faith in God had been restored. My ordeal had come to an end. Several men dressed in FBI uniforms had rescued me.

"You're going to be okay, ma'am," an agent said.

I was speechless. I wiped my eyes with my hands, as tears of joy started to flow. I knew I was fortunate to have survived to see this day.

It wasn't long before news vans and reporters were parked outside. I saw EMT workers load a stretcher with a body covered in a sheet onto an ambulance. Paramedics were hauling me away on a stretcher, pushing me toward a second ambulance. As they were lifting me into the back, insensitive reporters surrounded me, asking me lurid questions that I was in no mood to answer.

"Can we get a statement?" a male reporter asked.

"Stand back and make room," one EMT worker shouted to the reporters.

Once I was safely inside the ambulance, I asked the EMT worker to tell me the date.

She gave me a sad smile. "It's April 13, 2006, ma'am."

My jaw dropped. That meant I had been held in captivity for two years!

On my ride to the hospital, I was told that the man who had held me captive took his own life when FBI agents surrounded him. Instead of surrendering, he placed the barrel of a pistol inside his mouth and pulled the trigger.

* * * * *

Stanley came to visit me at Stony Brook Hospital. I was so happy to see him. He brought me flowers and a huge teddy bear.

I hadn't seen Stanley in what felt like an eternity. He had matured so much! We hugged, then he pulled away from me and filled me in on the details.

"They say that David and his parents were heavily involved in sex trafficking and that you were one of the lucky ones to have made it out alive."

"How many other survivors did they find?" I asked.

"Seven. David's family was already being watched by the FBI because his neighbors had complained about some odd behavior. That's how the sex ring was discovered. To get their time reduced, he and his parents are cooperating with the FBI to help find other surviving victims and to help convict other traffickers."

All I wanted to do was thank God that I was okay and reunited with Stanley.

June 11, 2008

Dear Diary,

After my story got out, I received many generous donations—enough to pay for my tuition at Suffolk County Community College. After two years of college, I obtained my associate's degree in social work. My goal was to rescue little boys and girls going through what my siblings and I had gone through.

Stanley stopped hanging out with the wrong crowd; he did not want to end up either dead or in jail. He graduated from high school, and now he is going to college to become a chemical dependency counselor. He said that drugs had ruined our family, so he had a passion to try to help other addicts clean up their act. For him, it was personal.

I still visit Emily every chance I get, and she still claims to see UFOs. She was never the same after Nancy died; she was not mentally stable, so the psychiatrist did not feel that releasing her would be a good idea.

It's strange, but during the last few nights before I was rescued, Tony appeared in my dreams to tell me that everything was going to be okay.

Every year, Stanley and I go to Tony's gravesite to wish him a happy birthday and give him fresh flowers. To this very day, I still feel his spirit watching over me—and Stanley will tell you the same.

About the Author

 Lloyd Williams is an African-American writer born and raised on Long Island, New York. Throughout his life he faced many obstacles in which he prevailed. His knack to tell heartfelt stories to his friends and family gave him inspiration to publish his work.

DATE DUE

GAYLORD			PRINTED IN U.S.A.

22662212R00065

Made in the USA
Middletown, DE
05 August 2015